A catalogue record for this book is available from the British Library

Published by Ladybird Books Ltd Loughborough Leicestershire UK
Ladybird Books Ltd is a subsidiary of the Penguin Group of companies
LADYBIRD and the device of a Ladybird are trademarks of Ladybird Books Ltd

Printed in Belgium

DISNEY
THE LITTLE
MERMAID

Ladybird

It was a very important day in the underwater kingdom of the merpeople. King Triton had invited all the sea creatures to a special concert. His youngest daughter, Princess Ariel, was sixteen years old, and she was going to sing for them.

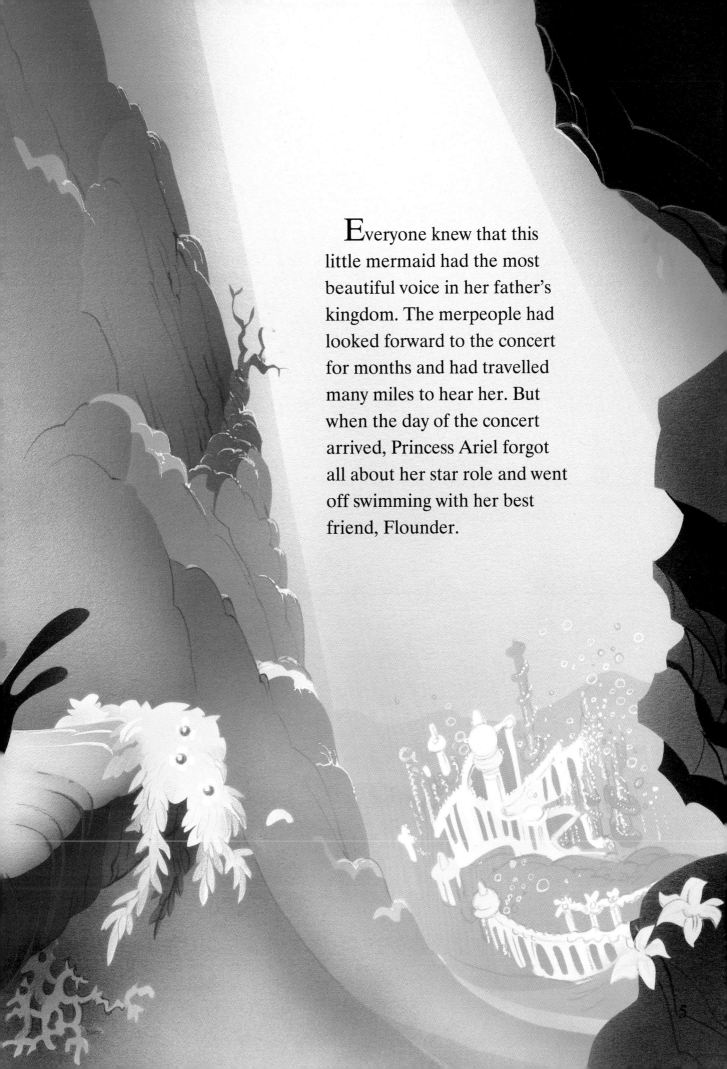

Everyone knew that this little mermaid had the most beautiful voice in her father's kingdom. The merpeople had looked forward to the concert for months and had travelled many miles to hear her. But when the day of the concert arrived, Princess Ariel forgot all about her star role and went off swimming with her best friend, Flounder.

5

The concert was already well under way in the Great Hall at the palace. Each of Ariel's six sisters introduced themselves to the audience, and everyone waited eagerly for the debut of the youngest princess… but she was nowhere to be found.

"My concert is ruined!" wailed Sebastian, the Royal Musical Director, holding his head in his claws.

King Triton was furious. "Ariel! Where has she got to?" he thundered, storming away.

Meanwhile, far from the commotion at the palace, Ariel was exploring the ruins of a sunken ship – a ship that had once belonged to the strange and wonderful world of humans.

"Oh, my! Have you ever seen anything so wonderful in your entire life?" gasped Ariel, picking up an object from the deck.

"What is it?" asked Flounder.

"I don't know… but I bet Scuttle will," Ariel replied. Suddenly, they heard a noise behind them.

"Ahhh!" squealed Flounder. "Sh… sh… sharks!"

He quickly followed Ariel through the ship's many rooms,
with the shark close behind them. They passed swiftly through
a narrow anchor ring. The shark was much too big to follow.

"You big bully!" shouted Flounder, now feeling very brave.
"You should be ashamed of yourself!"

Once the scare was over, Ariel and Flounder went to the surface in search of Scuttle. They found their seagull friend on a rock.

"Scuttle, look what we've found!" cried Ariel. She proudly held up the strange object from the sunken ship.

"Human stuff, eh?" said Scuttle wisely. "Let me see. This is special… very, very unusual."

"What is it?" giggled Ariel, excitedly.

"It's a dinglehopper," the expert on humans announced. "Humans use it for… um… combing their hair." Scuttle raised the fork to his head to demonstrate this, and started to hum cheerfully.

"Music!" gasped Ariel. "The concert! Oh, no… my father will kill me!" She dived quickly into the water.

13

Meanwhile, in a deeper, darker part of the ocean, Ursula the sea witch sat hugging her pet eels, Flotsam and Jetsam.

Many years ago, Ursula had been banished from Triton's palace and now she plotted her revenge. She followed the little mermaid's journey home through a crystal ball.

"I want to keep a close eye on this pretty little daughter of his… she may be the key to Triton's downfall."

Ariel stood before her father in the throne room. She had never seen him so angry. "I'm sorry," apologised Ariel, "I just forgot. I…"

But her father wouldn't listen. "As a result of your careless behaviour, the entire celebration was…"

"…completely ruined," continued Sebastian, who had hopped off the throne towards her.

"Silence!" screamed the King, as Flounder started to explain on Ariel's behalf. "You must never go to the surface again. Is that clear?"

"Do you think I was too hard on her?" asked Triton, turning regretfully to Sebastian once Ariel and Flounder had left.

"Definitely not. No, sir… I'd keep her under tight control."

"You're absolutely right, Sebastian. Ariel needs constant supervision," replied the King, brightening up a little. "And you are just the crab to do it!"

"How do I get myself into these situations?" groaned Sebastian as he wandered along the seabed looking for Ariel. "I should be writing symphonies, not running round after some headstrong teenager."

He found Ariel in a secret cave, surrounded by her human treasures.

The Musical Director was so busy watching Ariel that he forgot to look where he was walking. He tripped and fell heavily into the middle of the cave.

"Sebastian!" cried Ariel.

"What are you… how could you…?" said the crab, trying to appear important. "If your father knew about this place…"

Suddenly something passed above their heads casting a shadow over the cave. "A ship!" thought Ariel and, forgetting about Sebastian, she swam quickly to the surface.

Ariel had seen ships many times before, but never as close as this. Her eyes opened wide in astonishment.

Sailors were laughing merrily and dancing on the open deck. They were wishing *Happy Birthday!* to a very handsome young man, whose name was Prince Eric. Ariel watched the sailors present him with a large statue of himself.

They were having such a good time that they didn't seem to notice a large storm brewing overhead. Heavy raindrops started to fall and lightning lit up the whole sky.

Prince Eric tried to keep the ship on course but the wind was too strong. Then lightning struck the bow and the ship exploded. Eric was thrown into the sea. Ariel dived towards the Prince and dragged him to the shore.

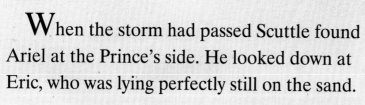

When the storm had passed Scuttle found Ariel at the Prince's side. He looked down at Eric, who was lying perfectly still on the sand.

"Is he dead?" asked Ariel weakly.

"It's hard to say," said Scuttle, putting his ear to the Prince's boot. "I can't make out a heartbeat – he must be dead."

"No, look! He's breathing," said Ariel. "Oh, he's so beautiful!" At that moment, Ariel knew she loved Eric. She began to sing softly and, all at once, she saw his eyelids flutter. Just as Eric opened his eyes, Ariel dived back into the sea. All he could remember was her beautiful voice.

29

When Ariel returned to her secret cave, she was delighted to find the statue of Eric, which Flounder had rescued from the sinking ship.

"Thank you, Flounder!" laughed Ariel. "It looks just like him."

Sebastian looked on helplessly from the edge of the cave. He was feeling very worried. He hadn't intended to tell King Triton about Eric. It had just slipped out accidentally.

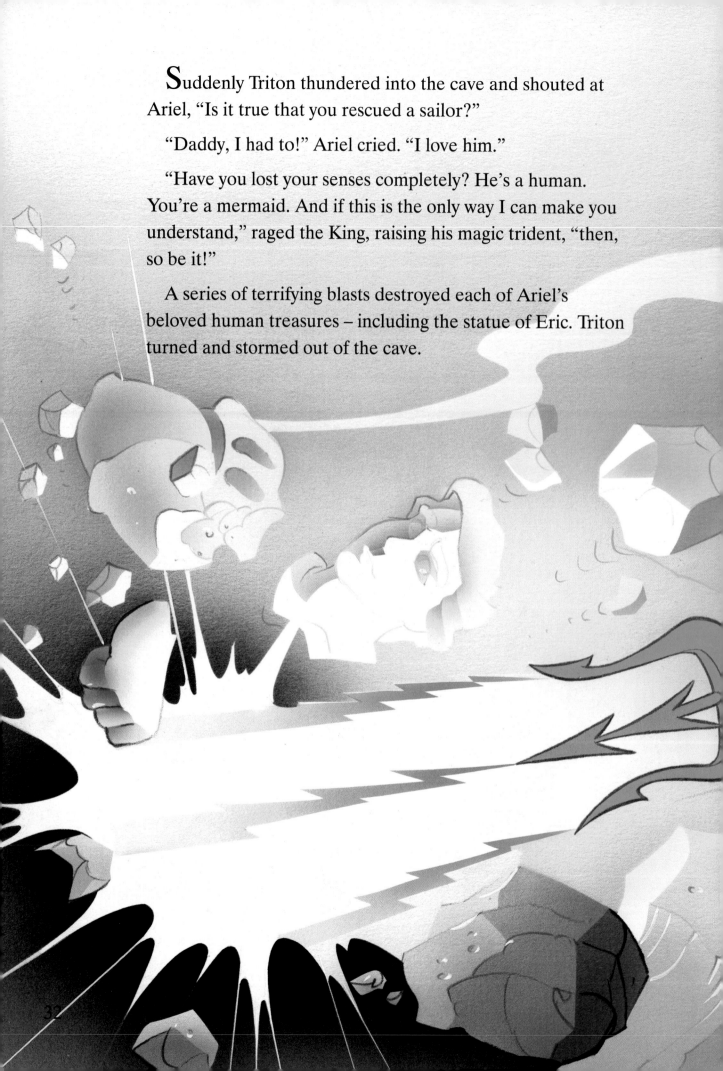

Suddenly Triton thundered into the cave and shouted at Ariel, "Is it true that you rescued a sailor?"

"Daddy, I had to!" Ariel cried. "I love him."

"Have you lost your senses completely? He's a human. You're a mermaid. And if this is the only way I can make you understand," raged the King, raising his magic trident, "then, so be it!"

A series of terrifying blasts destroyed each of Ariel's beloved human treasures – including the statue of Eric. Triton turned and stormed out of the cave.

Ariel sat weeping among her ruined possessions. Gradually she became aware of two dark shadows swimming around her. She raised her head to see two evil-looking eels.

"Who… who are you?" she sobbed.

"Don't be scared," replied one of the eels. "We know someone who can make all your dreams come true. Ursula the sea witch has great powers, you know."

Flotsam and Jetsam led Ariel to the sea witch's cavern. Ursula came straight to the point. "You're in love with a human, so you must become a human, too."

"Can you do that for me?" gasped Ariel.

"Of course," replied Ursula. A wicked smile crept across her ugly face. She moved closer to Ariel and gripped her tightly. "Once we have agreed the terms of the contract."

Ursula loosened her hold and looked straight at Ariel.

"In exchange for your voice, I will turn you into a human for three days. If Eric hasn't kissed you before sunset on the third day, you will become a mermaid again and belong to me for ever."

The sea witch held up a contract. "Do we have a deal?" she coaxed.

"No, Ariel, don't sign," begged Sebastian and Flounder, who had crept silently into the cavern. "Don't listen to her!"

Ariel hesitated.

"Make your choice!" snapped Ursula. "I'm a very busy woman and I haven't got all day."

Ariel signed the contract.

Ursula chanted a magic spell and Ariel was transformed into a human. She began to gasp for air, and Sebastian and Flounder pushed her to the surface, where she could breathe.

The next thing Ariel knew, she was up on the beach.

Scuttle flew down to say hello. "Hey!" he said. "Let me look at you, Ariel. There's something different about you, but I can't quite put my foot on it."

"She's got legs, you idiot!" explained Sebastian. "Ursula has turned Ariel into a human."

Further along the beach, Prince Eric was walking with his dog, Max. Since the day of the storm, Eric had often thought about the mysterious girl with the beautiful voice who had rescued him. Would he ever see her again?

Then he glanced up and saw someone behind a rock. His heart skipped a beat. It was the girl he'd been searching for!

"Um… excuse me," he asked, "but have we met before?"

Ariel nodded. Eric was disappointed when he realised that this girl could not speak. "You can't be the one I thought you were," he said sadly.

Prince Eric took Ariel back to the castle, where she was given plenty to eat and was dressed in fine clothes. Soon all the servants were talking about the beautiful but silent girl who combed her hair with a fork.

At the end of the day, Ariel returned to her luxurious bedroom. Sebastian, her faithful crab companion, climbed out of her pocket.

"Now, young lady," he said. "We need a plan to get Eric to kiss you. Tomorrow, you must look your best and…" Sebastian's voice trailed off. It was no use. Ariel wasn't listening.

The next morning, Eric took Ariel out for a ride to show her his kingdom.

Ariel was amazed by everything she saw. How she wished she could speak to Eric! She was certain he was falling in love with her, but he didn't try to kiss her once.

In the afternoon, Eric took Ariel out in a boat on a quiet lake. Everything was perfect. Ariel looked up at Eric and smiled. He leaned forward to kiss her, but suddenly Flotsam and Jetsam leapt from the lake and overturned the boat. Eric and Ariel fell into the water.

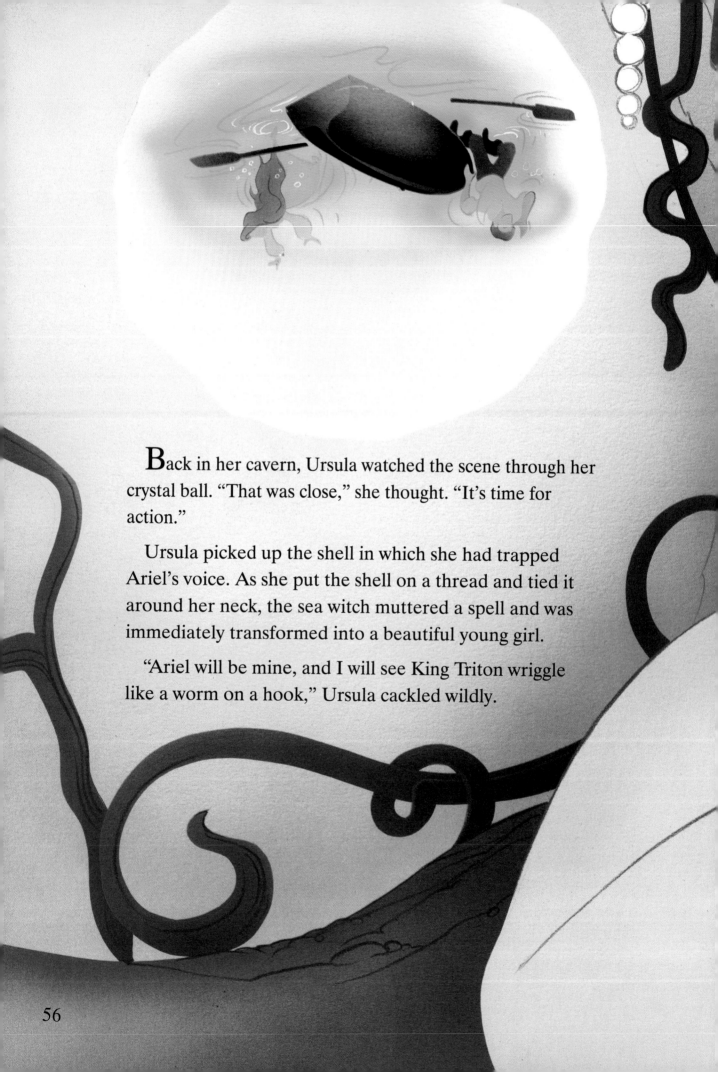

Back in her cavern, Ursula watched the scene through her crystal ball. "That was close," she thought. "It's time for action."

Ursula picked up the shell in which she had trapped Ariel's voice. As she put the shell on a thread and tied it around her neck, the sea witch muttered a spell and was immediately transformed into a beautiful young girl.

"Ariel will be mine, and I will see King Triton wriggle like a worm on a hook," Ursula cackled wildly.

Later that evening Eric went for a stroll along the beach. As he gazed wistfully out to sea, the sound of singing came drifting through the mist. It was *the voice!* He looked back to see a girl walking on the sand. Her shell necklace gleamed as she sang… and Eric was immediately entranced.

Eric returned to the castle and announced that he would marry the girl the very next day.

Grimsby, the Prince's Chancellor, gasped in disbelief. He knew he would have trouble preparing the wedding ship in time.

But the next day, after many hours hard work, the wedding ship set sail. Scuttle, who was flying high in the distance, saw the ship and decided to investigate. He could hear someone singing, and went closer to see who it was.

Peeping through a porthole, Scuttle saw Ursula's true reflection in a mirror. He hurried away to find Ariel.

On the shore, Ariel watched the brightly decorated wedding ship… and the sun lowering in the sky. She was heartbroken.

Suddenly, she heard Scuttle's excited voice. She could hardly believe what he said. "The Prince is marrying Ursula! She's in disguise."

Sebastian was horrified. "We've got to stop that wedding!" he exclaimed. "Flounder, you take Ariel to the ship. I'll fetch King Triton."

While Flounder pulled Ariel towards the ship on a barrel, Scuttle sounded the alarm. He called as many sea birds and other creatures as he could, and led the attack on the wedding. The guests scattered in confusion.

Scuttle headed straight for Ursula and snatched the necklace from her throat. The shell fell to the deck and shattered in pieces at Ariel's feet. The voice, now free, returned to its rightful owner.

"Eric," Ariel cried, and at once he came out of the trance.

Eric ran to Ariel and took her in his arms. "It was you all the time," he said. "You *are* the one who saved me!"

"Oh, Eric, I wanted to tell you," Ariel replied.

But before Eric could kiss her, the sun dipped below the horizon and Ariel was turned back into a mermaid.

Ursula, no longer in disguise, grabbed Ariel.

"So long, young Prince!" the sea witch shrieked triumphantly, disappearing into the sea.

An eerie silence filled the whole ship.

Eric took off his jacket and leapt straight into a small rowing boat. In his hands he carried a sharp harpoon.

Grimsby tried to stop Eric, but the Prince was determined. "I lost her once," he shouted. "I'm not going to lose her again."

Meanwhile, at the bottom of the sea, King Triton and Ursula met face to face to bargain over Ariel's freedom.

"Very well, Triton," said the sea witch, "I am willing to exchange your daughter for someone even better. Now, do we have a deal?" she sneered.

Triton had no choice. He changed the signature on the contract to his own and handed Ursula his magic trident.

Ursula beamed with happiness. "At last! It's all mine. I am the ruler of the ocean!" She pointed the trident at the King and transformed him into a slimy, helpless sea creature.

"You monster!" shouted Ariel, clawing wildly at her father's enemy.

"Don't fool with me," bellowed Ursula, throwing Ariel aside.

Suddenly Eric appeared. With a mighty heave he flung the harpoon towards Ursula, wounding her arm.

"Eric, look out!" cried Ariel, as the enraged sea witch aimed the magic trident at the Prince. Ariel dived towards Ursula and knocked her off balance. The trident blasted the evil eels, Flotsam and Jetsam, to pieces.

"Oh, my babies, my poor little poopsies!" wailed Ursula.

The sea witch's tears quickly turned to rage. The fury in her evil heart grew, and so did she, until at last she towered over the ocean.

"Ah… you pitiful fools!" she shrieked at Ariel and Eric. "You can't escape me now!"

Ursula turned the water into a raging whirlpool. Lightning flashed and great waves swept across the ocean. Shipwrecks that had lain for many years on the seabed were thrown to the surface.

Eric swam against the giant waves until, at last, he reached one of the dredged-up ships.

The Prince ran across the rolling deck and took control of
the ship's wheel. He aimed its pointed bow at the heart of the
swollen sea witch and charged forward. With a dreadful
scream, Ursula reeled backwards and disintegrated into a
pool of bubbling black ooze.

At last, Ursula was gone. The trident she had been holding sank beneath the waves. Triton touched it and became King once more.

The King granted Ariel her dearest wish, making her a human for ever. He and Sebastian watched her walk away with Eric. "I think I'm going to miss her," Ariel's father sighed.

A few days later, Eric and Ariel were married on board the wedding ship. King Triton proudly watched over them from the sea.

"I think they're going to live happily ever after," said Scuttle.

And for once, he was absolutely right!